Elizabeth's Stormy Ride

by Joanne Mattern
Illustrated by Craig Orback

HOUGHTON MIFFLIN HARCOURT
School Publishers

Printed in China

ISBN-10: 0-547-25343-5
ISBN-13: 978-0-547-25343-5

8 9 10 0940 18 17 16 15 14 13
4500396701

Thunder crashed. Lightning flashed. Rain poured down outside the cabin in the California mountains where Elizabeth and her family lived.

Mama lay on the bed, her face white with pain. Elizabeth's father had gone hunting. He would not be back for a week. Now the baby was coming, almost a month early.

Elizabeth was only 11 years old. What could she do?

Elizabeth's mother needs help.

Elizabeth goes out into the storm.

"Can you go for help?" Elizabeth's mother said. "I need Mrs. Baldwin from town."

Elizabeth nodded. Mrs. Baldwin delivered babies. She had delivered Elizabeth and her brothers and sisters.

"Go down the road and turn right at the big oak. Cross the river at the bridge. Turn left along the river. Mrs. Baldwin's house is after the stone wall."

Elizabeth went outside. Rain fell hard.

Elizabeth escorted Bessie, their horse, out of the barn. She climbed up into the saddle.

It made her feel good when her mother relied on her to do something important. What could be more important than getting help for Mama?

Elizabeth rides Bessie along the road.

Elizabeth sat straight and tall in the saddle. "I can do this," she said to herself.

Bessie was usually a calm horse. She trotted along the road. Just then, a clap of thunder shook the air. Bessie snorted and jumped. Elizabeth pulled back on the reins to steady her. "It's okay," she said.

Bessie paused and trotted on.

Elizabeth rode through the woods. The storm was making the road muddy. Suddenly, Bessie slipped. Elizabeth held tight as the horse steadied herself.

They came to a fork in the road. Elizabeth looked around. A big tree reached over the road. *Mama said I should turn right at the big tree,* she thought. Elizabeth guided Bessie to the right.

Elizabeth and Bessie come to a fork in the road.

Elizabeth and Bessie have to cross the bridge.

Soon they came to the bridge. "Oh, no!" Elizabeth cried. The rain had swelled the river and flooded the bridge.

Bessie stopped. Elizabeth shivered with fear. Would the water wash her away? Then she shook her head. "I must be brave because Mama needs me." She slapped the reins gently on Bessie's neck. "Let's go, Bessie," she said.

Elizabeth and Bessie carefully cross the bridge.

Bessie stepped forward. "She trusts me!"
Elizabeth said with pride. She held on tight.

The rough water washed over Bessie's feet
and splashed onto Elizabeth's long skirt. The
wind blew hard against them. It seemed to take
forever, but finally they crossed the bridge.

"Good girl!" Elizabeth said. She patted
Bessie's neck. But, it was getting dark, and she
began to worry.

Suddenly, Elizabeth stopped the horse. Another road crossed the one she was on. Which way would take her to town?

Elizabeth remembered her mother's words. *She had said to turn left and ride along the river.* That is what Elizabeth and Bessie did. It was getting harder to see in the dark. Finally she saw the stone wall, so she knew this was the right road.

Elizabeth sees the stone wall.

Suddenly, Bessie tripped. She recovered but then planted all four hooves firmly on the ground. The horse would not go any farther.

Bessie will not move.

"Come on, Bessie!" Elizabeth cried. She shook the reins. "We're almost there. Let's go!" But the horse stood still.

Elizabeth slid off the horse's back. She carefully lifted Bessie's right front foot and felt along the bottom of the hoof. Sure enough, there was a stone stuck in there. Elizabeth curled her fingers around the stone and pulled. The stone popped out.

Back in the saddle, Elizabeth slapped the reins and Bessie trotted on. Soon they could see houses ahead of them. They were almost there!

Elizabeth found the right house. She tied Bessie to the fence and ran to the door. She knocked loudly.

"Mrs. Baldwin," she cried. "Come quickly!"

A middle-aged woman opened the door. "What's wrong?" she asked.

"The baby is coming early! My mother needs you right away!"

Elizabeth tells Mrs. Baldwin about her mother.

Mrs. Baldwin quickly got her horse, and Elizabeth led the way back to the mountain cabin.

Mrs. Baldwin ran inside while Elizabeth and her brother John took Bessie to the barn. The horse deserved some attention after her tough ride. When Elizabeth and John walked out of the barn, the storm had passed and the moon was rising.

Mrs. Baldwin came outside. "It's a boy," she said with a big smile. "He's fine. So is his mother."

Mrs. Baldwin tells Elizabeth that she is brave.

Mrs. Baldwin put a hand on Elizabeth's shoulder. "You're worthy of great praise," she said. "You did a brave thing today."

"Thank you," Elizabeth said. "At first I didn't think I could do it. Now I know I can! Mama and Papa can always count on me."

Responding

✔ **TARGET SKILL** **Compare and Contrast**

How did Elizabeth's feelings differ before and after her ride? Copy and complete the chart below.

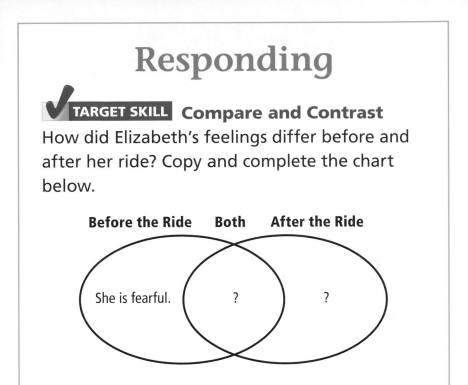

Before the Ride   **Both**   **After the Ride**

She is fearful.   ?   ?

✏ Write About It

Text to Text Think of another story where the hero or heroine had to overcome his or her fears to solve a problem. Write a descriptive paragraph showing what this character did to solve the problem. Include how the character got over his or her fears.